I Want To Be BACON When I Grow Up!

FARMER TIM'S HAPPY PIG
AND
OTHER YUMMY THINGS FARM

Hi, there! Welcome to Farmer Tim's Happy Pig and Other Yummy Things Farm. Do you see the mamma pig and her piglets?

For lunch, Farmer Tim gave them nice yummy carrots, apples, and other delicious goodies that every child, including you, should eat.

When they finished eating, Mamma Pig asked her little piggies what they wanted to be when they grew up.

That was a good question, a question none of the little piggies had ever considered. So they got real quiet and began to think. What would they be? In this day and age, a pig could be anything it wanted to be. So they thought and they pondered and they wondered what they would grow up to be.

Sister Pig didn't have to think for too long. She had really BIG dreams of reaching for the stars. She cleared her throat and declared, "I want be an astronaut. I'll be the first pig in space!"

She knew that monkeys, dogs, and
even humans had already gone, so why
not her? She felt that among the stars
is where she belonged.

Brother Pig had another idea. He was the big brother and was used to being in charge. But don't worry, he wasn't a bully. He just liked to tell everyone what to do.

He said, "I will become the president of the United States!" And while he didn't know much about politics, he thought he would enjoy the mudslinging part. After all, mud is awesome. In fact, he already had the perfect slogan, "It's time for swine!"

Melvin was the baby pig of the litter and he was excited to tell them what he wanted to be. He was going to be something awesome. He wanted to be something great.

He told them, "I want to become something that will make the world a better place. When I grow up I want to be..."

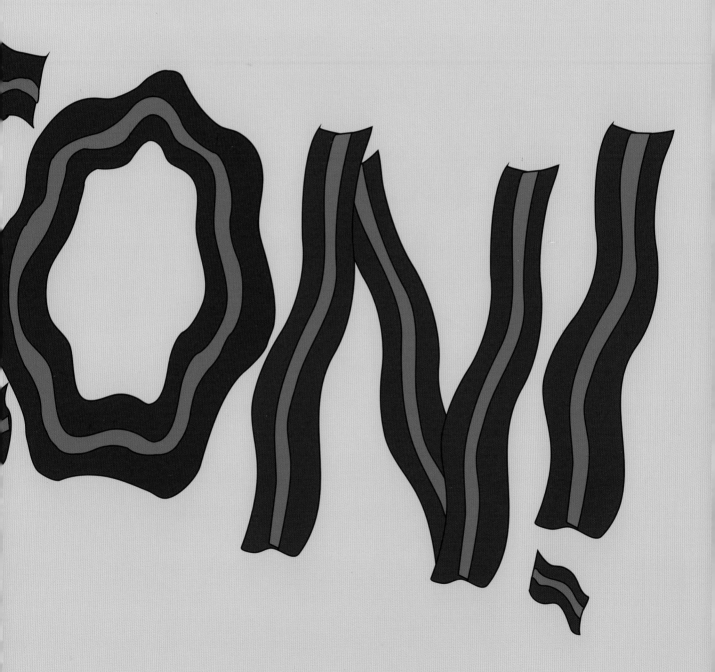

There were many reasons why Melvin wanted to be bacon. Pizza was one of them. Everyone loves pizza. It's great for parties or when watching sports.

Pizza is a place where tasty mushrooms and pepperoni sit side-by-side in perfect harmony. And while pizza is yum, everyone knows that bacon on your pizza is YUM YUM!

Let's not forget about breakfast. They say it's the most important meal of the day. Melvin didn't know who 'they' were, but they made a lot of sense.

A well-balanced meal didn't have to be boring. Eggs were good and all, but eggs with bacon was the best way to start the day!

At this point, a doubtful Sister Pig interrupted and asked, "Um...Melvin, you do know where bacon comes from, right?"

Melvin knew, and he was all right with it. He said, "All food comes from somewhere and needs to be respected, but people have to eat! And tasty food helps that happen!"

An example of a tasty food is a hamburger. Throw some crisp lettuce and a juicy tomato on it and you're close to perfection. Oh, and a pickle! Now you're looking good, but let's get real. A burger without bacon is like a joke without laughter. Just plain sad.

In fact, there were many examples of tasty foods made even tastier with bacon: salads, shrimp, chili cheese fries, cupcakes, turkey legs, hotdogs, sandwiches, baked potatoes, and much, much more. The list of things that bacon made better could go on and on forever and three days and two hours and twenty-two minutes.

Mamma Pig was proud of her son for wanting to make the lives of people better. Laughingly, she said, "It's great that you want to be bacon, Melvin. But you do know that not all foods have bacon on them."

Melvin smiled and winked,
"Maybe, but the good ones do!"

THE
END

Now that the story is over,

let's play some games.

Go local sports team!

Can you find these things?

 Apple

 Cupcake

 9 Sheep

 Salad

 Burger

 5 Stars

 Cocktail Sausage

 Top Hat

 4 Strips of bacon

 Baked Potato

Look and Find

Spot Seven Differences

Spot Seven Differences

1. Brother Pig's eye 2. Buckle on hat 3. Flower picture is different
4. Tassel missing from left flag 5. Mug on desk 6. Extra star in right flag 7. Cloud

10 Bacon facts
(That you can take to the piggy bank)

1. Bacon tastes good.

2. People who like bacon are usually awesome.
People who do not like bacon might be awesome too,
but there are no guarantees.

3. To make turkey bacon taste more like real bacon, you need to
wrap it in bacon.

4. At least one pound of bacon was eaten during the making of
this book.

5. No one in real life has ever broken into a song
and dance number about bacon, but with this book,
we are one step closer to that reality.

6. It's not possible to eat 500 pounds of bacon in one hour.

7. Whenever I think about bacon, I get hungry.

8. The word bacon starts with the letter 'B',
but ends with the letter 'N'.

9. If people had a choice between getting poked in the eye or
getting a piece of bacon, most would choose the bacon.

10. Bacon is not considered a fruit.

Look Out For These
Upcoming Titles:

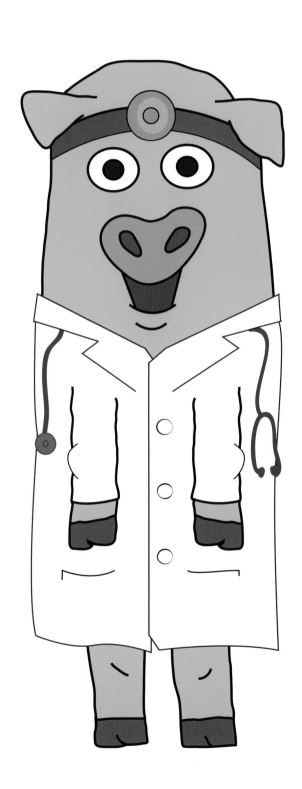

Alright, readers, it's goodbye for real this time.
Don't forget to eat your fruits and vegetables
because bacon is only PART of a balanced diet!